SOWING *in* FAMINE

Dr. Rodney M. Howard-Browne

RMI PUBLICATIONS
P.O. Box 292888 • Tampa, FL 33687 • USA

Sowing in Famine

ISBN 1-884662-09-6

Published by RMI Publications
P.O. Box 292888 • Tampa, FL 33687 • USA
Published in the United States of America

Unless otherwise indicated, all scriptural references are from the King James Version of the BIBLE.

Scripture portions marked "Amp" are taken from The Amplified Bible, copyright © 1987 by the Zondervan Corporation.

ONE

SOWING SEED *in* A TIME *of* FAMINE

The following scriptures tell the story of Isaac, a man who sowed seed in a time of famine and received a hundredfold return on his seed in the same year.

Genesis 26:1 *And there was a famine in the land, beside the first famine that was in the days of Abraham. And Isaac went unto Abimelech king of the Philistines unto Gerar.*

Genesis 26:12-14 *Then Isaac sowed in that land, and received in the same year an hundredfold: and the LORD blessed him. And the man waxed great, and went forward, and grew until he became very great: For he had possession of flocks, and possession of herds, and* *great store of servants: and the Philistines envied him.*

SOWING *in* THE LAND *in* THE YEAR OF DROUGHT CAUSES GOD'S PROVISION

If you think about it, no one in his right mind sows seed in a time of famine. A farmer knows that during a time of drought, the ground is dry and dusty, and plowing and sowing seed under these conditions can cause one of three things to happen. The first thing that could happen is that the wind could blow away the topsoil, then the seed. The second thing is that rains could finally come and wash away the topsoil and the seed, and leave terrible erosion. The third thing that could happen is that the seed will just remain in the ground, never producing.

In this scripture passage, we see Isaac sowing seed in the land during a time of famine. This shows us that when God's blessing is upon your life, you will see miraculous supernatural provision regardless of the conditions of life around you.

TWO

MY TESTIMONY *when* GENESIS 26 BECAME A REALITY TO ME

This scripture first became a reality to me in 1982. I had started out in full-time ministry in 1980 and in October of 1981, Adonica and I were married. We began our married life together traveling and ministering across Southern Africa.

When we married, the only thing I owned (besides my clothes and suitcase) was a guitar and all she had was a motorcar. I jokingly tell everyone that was the reason I married her. The automobile we had was fine for a single person driving around the city every day, but it was not the best thing to have when it came to loading luggage and traveling around South Africa. It was a small sports car that could move fast on a flat road, but it had a hard time going uphill. It kept breaking down with one sort of problem or another and was costing us a lot of money.

One night as we were driving down the highway, the car broke down once again. I was so frustrated that I got out and left the car on the side of the highway and never went back. We called our next-door neighbor and told her that if she wanted the car, she could have it. We gave her the address where we had left it and told her that all she had to do was to fetch it from where we had left it and it was hers. She was a Jewish girl and we had been witnessing to her. We figured that she would have a whole car for only the price of fixing it. Her father came to meet us, because he had never heard of people who would give away a whole car!

WE WERE AT *the* BOTTOM *of* THE BARREL

Here we were, traveling evangelists, with very little money (less than 200 rands) and no car. We definitely felt like we were in a time of famine. Not only were we at the bottom of the barrel, we felt like the barrel was on top of us! During the course of that week, we happened to be attending a convention and that night, guess what the preacher preached on. "Sowing in famine!"

Initially, I was not a happy camper. I felt that the message was aimed right at me. The Holy Spirit was dealing with my flesh and the longer the speaker preached, the more I realized that I had nothing to lose. We needed to give. Yes, even the little we had at the time. We had to step out of the boat and walk on the water of the supernatural. Adonica and I decided to sow almost all the money, except a few rands. We made up our minds to believe God for a supernatural breakthrough.

The scripture says that Isaac sowed seed in

the land in the time of famine, not just in the time of abundance. Many people refuse to give when they are having a difficult time financially. They try to hang on to what they have. God tells us to do the opposite-to sow seed in our time of need! Isaac received a hundredfold and the Lord blessed him and he grew great and was blessed with large numbers of flocks and herds and servants, and the Philistines envied him.

STEPPING OUT *in* FAITH

That night we sowed, believing God for a miracle, which is what we desperately needed. The next Sunday a pastor we knew told me of a gentleman in his church who managed a car dealership. This gentleman had heard of our plight and wanted to help. I was a little embarrassed by this and said to the pastor, "Please, I can't go see him because I don't have any money and he is probably going to want a down payment. I am not in a position to do anything at this time." The pastor assured me that this man wanted to help and it would not hurt me to go see him.

THIS *is* YOUR CAR

The next afternoon we met the gentleman at his dealership and he took my wife and me into his office. He told us that before we looked at any other vehicles, he had a vehicle we should test-drive. We headed off down the road in the car and while we were driving, the Spirit of the Lord said these words to me, "This is your car." I asked Adonica, "Honey, how do you like this car?" She answered, "Please don't go buy the first car you drive. The man has plenty of other cars on the lot. Let's go look at different ones and then choose one."

"Honey, you don't understand what I mean," I explained. "The Lord has spoken to me and told me that this is our car." She just looked at me with those trusting brown eyes and told me that she did like the car.

When we arrived back at the dealership, the gentleman approached us and asked, "Do you like the car?" We unanimously replied that we did. Then he said, "The car is yours. It belonged to my wife and it was for sale, but the Lord told me to bless you and give it to you."

We were beside ourselves with joy as we headed off down the road in our new car! The car was worth a hundredfold of the amount we had sowed in famine and we had received our return in that same week! I have never forgotten that event and I still use this principle of sowing today (even, and especially, in hard times) both in my personal life and in the ministry.

THREE

the PROPHET, *the* RAVENS, *and the* WIDOW

Another passage that refers to sowing in famine and God's miraculous supernatural provision in a time of famine is found in **1 Kings 17:1-16.**

Vs. 1 *And Elijah the Tishbite, who was of the inhabitants of Gilead, said unto Ahab, As the LORD God of Israel liveth, before whom I stand, there shall not be dew nor rain these years, but according to my word.*
Vs. 2 *And the word of the LORD came unto him, saying,*
Vs. 3 *Get thee hence, and turn thee eastward, and hide thyself by the brook Cherith, that is*

before Jordan.
Vs. 4 *And it shall be, that thou shalt drink of the brook; and I have commanded the ravens to feed thee there.*
Vs. 5 *So he went and did according unto the word of the LORD: for he went and dwelt by the brook Cherith, that is before Jordan.*
Vs. 6 *And the ravens brought him bread and flesh in the morning, and bread and flesh in the evening; and he drank of the brook.*
Vs. 7 *And it came to pass after a while, that the brook dried up, because there had been no rain in the land.*
Vs. 8 *And the word of the LORD came unto him, saying,*
Vs. 9 *Arise, get thee to Zarephath, which belongeth to Zidon, and dwell there: behold, I have commanded a widow woman there to sustain thee.*
Vs. 10 *So, he arose and went to Zarephath. And when he came to the gate of the city, behold, the widow woman was there gathering sticks: and he called to her, and said, Fetch me, I pray thee, a little water in a vessel, that I may*

drink.

Vs. 11 *And as she was going to fetch it, he called to her, and said, Bring me, I pray thee, a morsel of bread in thine hand.*

Vs. 12 *And she said, As the LORD thy God liveth, I have not a cake, but an handful of meal in a barrel, and a little oil in a cruse: and, behold, I am gathering two sticks, that I may go in and dress it for me and my son, that we may eat it, and die.*

Vs. 13 *And Elijah said unto her, Fear not; go and do as thou hast said: but make me thereof a little cake first, and bring it unto me, and after make for thee and for thy son.*

Vs. 14 *For thus saith the LORD God of Israel, The barrel of meal shall not waste, neither shall the cruse of oil fail, until the day that the LORD sendeth rain upon the earth.*

Vs. 15 *And she went and did according to the saying of Elijah: and she, and he, and her house, did eat many days.*

Vs. 16 *And the barrel of meal wasted not, neither did the cruse of oil fail, according to the word of the LORD, which he spake by Elijah.*

GOD USES *the* MOST UNLIKELY VESSELS

In this passage of scripture, we see that the prophet Elijah prophesied that there would be a famine in the land. The Lord had a place of provision for the prophet and told him to go to the brook Cherith. God said He had commanded the ravens to feed him there. God commanded the ravens! God will make a way for you in the time of famine even if He has to command a scavenger to feed you. Could this mean that the only prerequisite you need in order to be used of God is to have a birdbrain?

When the brook dried up, God told the prophet to go to Zarephath where He had commanded a widow woman to provide for him. I don't know about you, but if this were me, I think I would be suffering from an inferiority complex by now. First the ravens, now a widow woman. You would think that God would have commanded a millionaire to feed His prophet, instead of a poor widow woman who was on her final meal. However, God was sending the prophet to the widow not to rob her, but to bring her into a place of supernatural abundant provision. God was about to provide for both the prophet and the widow, because of her obedience and willingness to share her last bit of food.

PLACING A DEMAND CAUSES A RELEASE *of* GOD'S PROVISION

Asking the widow for just a drink of water was a valid request from a stranger, but the prophet went a step further and asked for something to eat. The widow came back with the reply that she had only a little oil and a little meal. She was gathering some sticks to make a fire and then she was going to bake some little cakes so that she and her son could eat and then die. What a bleak future they had-but God had made a way for her. Elijah told her that she must do as she had said, but requested that she bring him something to eat first.

You can imagine what would have happened

if the media had gotten hold of this story. I can just see the headlines now: PREACHER ROBS WOMAN OF FINAL MEAL!

The widow did as Elijah said and I Kings 17:16 says that the jar of meal did not fail and the cruse of oil did not run out until the day the Lord sent rain on the earth. During this time of famine, Elijah, the widow, and her household ate and were fed supernaturally by God.

As you read further, you see that the widow's son died, but the prophet raised him up from the dead. This faithful woman came into God's miraculous supernatural provision.

God is in the multiplication business-a little becomes much when you put it in the Master's Hand.

FOUR

GOD'S PROVISION MANIFESTED *in* AFRICA

From December 1 through 5, 1997, we went back to the city of my birth, Port Elizabeth, in the Cape Province of South Africa. This was the first time we had been back in about six years. We went to minister at the church where I was raised as a child and it was wonderful to see friends and loved ones after so long a time. It was also interesting to see certain people who had known me from the time I was five years of age. The building was packed every night with about 2500 people, who came from all over South Africa.

THE BREAKTHROUGH COMES

In the morning service on Thursday, December 4, 1997, I called an African Anglican lay preacher forward and questioned him about the touch he had received from the Lord during that week. He was very excited, because the Lord had so wonderfully transformed his life. He kept saying, "I will never be the same again." He had purchased eight of our videos and someone had given him five more. He was beside himself with joy!

This pastor told me that he had a double garage on his house and he was going to invite his whole small town to come view the videos with him. I asked him how much it would cost to build a church building in his town. He replied that he thought it would cost around R20 000.

I felt prompted by the Holy Spirit to give him R5 000 from our ministry, then I opened up the opportunity for others in the service to give an offering to him. The response was overwhelming. People rushed to the altar while he stood crying and saying, "I can't believe this is happening!" The offering was R24 500. This was the second offering of the morning and this amount was outstanding for this part of the country. In the newspapers that morning, we had just read that the police cars were out of gasoline and the state had no money to buy more gas for the police vehicles.

Thursday night, the last evening service of the series of meetings, I saw something quite unlike anything I had ever seen before. We still had a meeting on Friday morning before climbing on board a flight bound for the U.S. On Thursday night, I taught the message "Sowing in Famine." As we were receiving the offering, the people began to shout, "Jesus! Jesus! Jesus!" as they worshipped the Lord with high praise. They would not stop. The offering was about R68 000, which once again was totally outstanding for that region of the nation. The people became totally set free in their giving. They grasped the fact that God desired to bless them and that they could be a blessing. What you need to realize is that

South Africans do not receive any tax deduction for their giving at all.

GIVING AS *an* ACT *of* WORSHIP

As the people continued to shout and worship God of their own accord, one person walked forward and laid money on the platform at the front of the building. Suddenly, hundreds of other people, without being asked, came and began to place money upon the altar. They did this one by one, until another R8 000 had been received. The ushers came and took the offering away, and what transpired next blew me away.

A young African gentleman removed his tie and laid it on the altar. I sat on the piano bench and just wept as the people, of their own accord, came and laid down their shoes, watches, jewelry, coats, sweaters, shirts, belts and other personal effects. They even brought surfboards, musical instruments and golf clubs. This went on for about an hour and a half. The altar was piled up with their giving, about 3½ feet high, right across the front of the platform. I had never seen giving like this before. There was such freedom in the place, and a joyful spirit filled the people as they came forward, rejoicing and worshipping with pure hearts.

The TESTIMONIES BEGIN *to* COME IN

Testimonies began to come in almost immediately during the service. When the young man who gave the surfboard got back to his seat, a person tapped him on the shoulder and told him to come over to the surf shop in the morning and pick out any new board that he chose.

We found out later that a woman who was raised as a Jehovah's Witness and had recently been saved was in the meeting. She attended this Pentecostal church, but was not Spirit-filled because she had a problem entering into the things of the Spirit due to her background. She was a surfer, and when the young man gave his surfboard, it totally blew her away. Realizing what that surfboard must have meant to him, she broke down and wept, and as she did, she was instantly filled with the Spirit. God touched her through giving.

Another gentleman came forward and testified that his wife had had a problem with giving in the past, but she had come forward to give R50 that night. The moment she got back to her seat, someone handed them R500! During that service, I prophesied that a spirit of giving would break out as never before, flowing across South Africa.

The next offering was an offering of people flocking to the altar to surrender their lives to Jesus and to rededicate their lives to Him. The altar was filled with the fourth and final offering of the night-and the most important offering-people! Testimonies are still pouring in from all over the Cape Province as a result of this week of meetings. At the Friday morning service, as a ministry, we were able to sow about R50 000 worth of videos into the lives of every individual at that meeting.

The Weekend Post, one of the area's leading newspapers, interviewed us that week and wanted to know all about the revival and what God was doing. Some of their reporters had also attended a number of the meetings. The newspaper headlines that weekend read:

HUNDREDS TAKE OFF THEIR CLOTHES *in* PORT ELIZABETH CHURCH!

Generally, it turned out to be a very positive article about the ministry and the revival. You can imagine that everyone wanted to buy that paper to find out why people removed their clothes in church!

The national news radio picked up the story and ran it as a news article. One of the leading Christian magazines, *Joy*, which is sold in bookstores nationwide, picked up the article on the revival and ran it as a feature.

We heard that a church of about 400 people in Cape Town received a freewill offering of R165 000 that Sunday. That is a totally supernatural occurrence in any country! As we climbed aboard the South African Airways 747 headed for Miami, Florida, I knew that I had witnessed a breakthrough in giving in the city and land of my birth.

FIVE

GOD'S PROVISION MANIFESTED *in the* U.S.

We landed in Tampa, Florida, on Saturday morning and spent the day resting and getting ready for Sunday morning at The River. I could never have imagined what was about to happen at church that Sunday.

The worship at The River that Sunday was awesome. I preached a message called "The River of God" and about sixty people responded to the altar call for salvation. Just prior to laying hands on everyone who desired prayer, which is our custom every Sunday, there was a pause in the service. There was a lull of about two minutes as we waited on God. Suddenly someone approached the altar and placed money on the altar, just as the people had in Africa. For about an hour and a half, they flooded the platform with everything from money to watches, jewelry, coats, musical instruments, ties and shoes.

My daughter Kelly placed her brand new, favorite jacket on the altar. While she did it she was weeping and I knew that God was dealing with her in a special way. I called her up to sing and she led the congregation in worship for about 15 minutes. Then with no one to catch her, she suddenly fell over backwards and lay on the floor trembling under the power of God.

GIVING CAUSES HEALING *in* ANOTHER STATE

One gentleman, who had a two-week-old son, brought an offering that morning. He did not know it, but that same morning his son, who was in another state, had been rushed into intensive care with serious complications in his lungs. He and his wife determined later that at the same time he gave the gift, his boy began to recover and was discharged the next day. The Sunday morning service finished at 3:40 on Sunday afternoon. It was a blowout! With testimony after testimony, people declared that God is indeed moving in a supernatural way in this day and hour! What He is doing is awesome.

The very next week, we closed out our crusade schedule for 1997. We conducted our last week of meetings, for the year, in the Florida Panhandle.

A PASTOR SET FREE *from* TRADITION

A pastor attended one of our services on a Friday night. He had been raised in a traditional Pentecostal denomination that taught that God wanted you to suffer and that God wanted you poor. He was suffering from problems in his kidneys and prostate. I called him forward for prayer and the pain left his body and he was healed by the power of God. I then felt led to give him $1000 and he broke down and wept. People in the congregation came forward and placed money in his hand. It was awesome! The next day he told me that he had been awake all night wrestling with the thought of receiving that offering. He then told me that the Lord had spoken to him, "Son, if I can't wash your feet, then you have no part of Me." This changed his life! On Saturday morning in the anointing service, we again witnessed what we had seen in Port Elizabeth and Tampa. A man came up to the altar and placed his and his wife's wedding rings on the altar as seed for sowing in famine. That started a stream of people coming forward to give something to Jesus.

You CAN BREAK THROUGH JUST LIKE *these* PEOPLE

You might be reading this book, thinking, "That's fine, but what does that have to do with me?" The Lord told me that in order to go to another level in Him, we need to get rid of the heavy loads we carry. The hot air balloonist, when wanting to go higher, throws off sandbags in order to gain altitude.

What do you want to see happen in your marriage, your job, your personal life, or even your ministry? Will everything stay the same or do you want to change?

How high you go in God is really up to you. It is not for the fainthearted, but for those who are radical and are willing to get out of the boat and walk on the water of the supernatural!

I trust that this teaching and these testimonies are a blessing to you and that you will realize that revival, when it comes, will come to every area of your life.

If this mini-book has touched your life in the area of sowing and reaping and the Lord speaks to your heart to sow a special seed into Revival Ministries International, be a part. Together, we are making an ETERNAL DIFFERENCE. If you feel led to partner with us, please, visit www.Revival.com and click on INVEST NOW or mail us at:

Revival Ministries International
P.O. Box 292888
Tampa, Florida 33687
USA

Telephone 813.971.9999
Fax 813.971.0701
www.revival.com

The River at Tampa Bay Church
The First River Fest, January 2013

The River at Tampa Bay Church
River Fest, February 2013

The River at Tampa Bay Church
River Fest, August 2013

The River at Tampa Bay Church
Thanksgiving Fest, November 2013

Revival Ministries International
Campmeeting Lakeland Summer 2013

The River at Tampa Bay Church
The Main Event, May 2014

The River at Tampa Bay Church
The Main Event, September 2013

The River at Tampa Bay Church
Easter Sunday, April 2014

The River at Tampa Bay Church
The Main Event, May 2014

About

Drs. Rodney and Adonica Howard-Browne

Drs. Rodney and Adonica Howard-Browne are the founders of Revival Ministries International, The River at Tampa Bay Church, River Bible Institute, River School of Worship, and River School of Government in Tampa, Florida.

Rodney and Adonica have been called by God to reach out to the nations – whilst keeping America as their primary mission field. Their heart is to see the Church – the Body of Christ – revived, and the lost won to Christ. They have conducted a number of mass crusades and many outreaches, but their heart is also to train and equip others to bring in the harvest – from one-on-one evangelism to outreaches that reach tens, hundreds, thousands and even tens of thousands. Every soul matters and every salvation is a victory for the kingdom of God!

In December of 1987, Rodney, along with his wife, Adonica, and their three children, Kirsten, Kelly and Kenneth, moved from their native land, South Africa, to the United States – called by God as missionaries from Africa to America. The Lord had spoken through Rodney in a word of prophecy and declared: "As America has sown missionaries over the last 200 years, I am going to raise up people from other nations to come to the United States of America. I am sending a mighty revival to America."

In April of 1989, the Lord sent a revival of signs and wonders and miracles that began in a church in Clifton Park, New York, that has continued until today, resulting in thousands of people being touched and changed as they encounter the presence of the living God! God is still moving today – saving, healing, delivering, restoring, and setting free!

Drs. Rodney and Adonica's second daughter, Kelly, was born with an incurable lung disease called Cystic Fibrosis. This demonic disease slowly destroyed her lungs. Early on Christmas morning 2002, at the age of eighteen, she ran out of lung capacity and breathed out her last breath. They placed her into the arms of her Lord and Savior and then vowed a vow. First, they vowed that the devil would pay for what he had done to their family. Secondly, they vowed to do everything in their power, with the help of the Lord, to win 100 million souls to Jesus and to put $1 billion into world missions and the harvest of souls.

With a passion for souls and a passion to revive and mobilize the body of Christ, Drs. Rodney and Adonica have conducted soul-winning efforts throughout America and other countries with "Good News" campaigns, R.M.I. Revivals, and the Great Awakening Tours (G.A.T.). As a result, millions have come to Christ and tens of thousands of believers have been revived and mobilized to preach the Gospel of Jesus Christ. So far, around the world, over 12,100,000 people have made decisions for Jesus Christ through this ministry.

Drs. Rodney and Adonica thank God for America and are grateful to have become Naturalized Citizens of the United States of America. When they became U.S. citizens, in 2008 and 2004 respectively, they took the United States Oath of Allegiance, which declares, "... I will support and defend the Constitution and laws of the United States of America against all enemies, foreign and domestic…" They took this oath to heart and intend to keep it. They love America, are praying for this country, and are trusting God to see another Great Awakening sweep across this land. Truly, the only hope for America is another Great Spiritual Awakening. For more information about the ministry of Drs. Rodney and Adonica Howard-Browne, please, visit www.revival.com

Other Books and Resources:

Books

This Present Glory
The Touch of God
The Reality of Life After Death
Seeing Jesus as He Really Is
The Curse Is Not Greater than the Blessing
The Coat My Father Gave Me
How to Increase and Release the Anointing
School of the Spirit
The Anointing
Fresh Oil from Heaven
Manifesting the Holy Ghost

Audio CDs

The Touch of God: The Anointing
Good News New York
Knowing the Person of the Holy Spirit
Prayer Time
Stewardship
The Love Walk by Dr. Adonica Howard-Browne
Weapons of Our Warfare
Becoming One Flesh by Drs. Rodney & Adonica Howard-Browne
Faith
Flowing in the Holy Ghost
How to Hear the Voice of God
How to Flow in the Anointing
Igniting the Fire
In Search of the Anointing
Prayer that Moves Mountains
Running the Heavenly Race
The Holy Spirit, His Purpose & Power
The Power to Create Wealth
Walking in Heaven's Light
All These Blessings

A Surplus of Prosperity
The Joy of the Lord Is My Strength
Prayer Secrets
Communion – The Table of the Lord
My Roadmap
My Mission – My Purpose
My Heart
My Family
My Worship
Decreeing Faith
Ingredients of Revival
Fear Not
Matters of the Heart by Dr. Adonica Howard-Browne
My Treasure
My Absolutes
My Father
My Crowns
My Comforter & Helper
Renewing the Mind
Seated in High Places
Triumphant Entry
Merchandising and Trafficking the Anointing
My Prayer Life
My Jesus
Seeing Jesus as He Really Is
Exposing the World's System
Living in the Land of Visions & Dreams

DVDs

God's Glory Manifested through Special Anointings
Good News New York
Jerusalem Ablaze
The Mercy of God by Dr. Adonica Howard-Browne
Are You a Performer or a Minister?
Revival at ORU Volume 1
Revival at ORU Volume 2

Revival at ORU Volume 3
The Realms of God
Singapore Ablaze
The Coat My Father Gave Me
Have You Ever Wondered What Jesus Was Like?
There Is a Storm Coming (Recorded live from Good News New York)
Budapest, Hungary Ablaze
The Camels Are Coming
Power Evangelism by Dr. Rodney Howard-Browne & The Great Awakening Team
Taking Cities in the Land of Giants
Renewing the Mind
Triumphant Entry
Merchandising and Trafficking the Anointing
Doing Business with God

Music
Nothing Is Impossible
Nothing Is Impossible Soundtrack
By His Stripes
Run with Fire
The Sweet Presence of Jesus
Eternity with Kelly Howard-Browne
Live from the River
You're Such a Good God to Me
Revival Down Under
Howard-Browne Family Christmas
Haitian Praise
He Lives
No Limits
Anointed – The Decade of the '80s

Connect

Please, visit revival.com for our latest updates and news. Many of our services are live online. Additionally, many of our recorded services are available on Video on Demand.

For a listing of Drs. Rodney and Adonica Howard-Browne's products and itinerary, please, visit revival.com

To download the soul-winning tools for free, please, visit revival.com and click on Soul-winning Tools or go to www.revival.com/soulwinning-tools.24.1.html

www.facebook.com/pages/Rodney-Adonica-Howard-Browne/31553452437

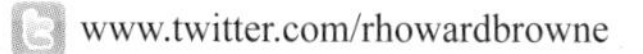

www.twitter.com/rhowardbrowne

www.youtube.com/rodneyhowardbrowne

www.instagram.com/rodneyhowardbrowne

The River at Tampa Bay Church

Pastors Rodney and Adonica Howard-Browne
(Senior Pastors & Founders)

Address: 3738 River International Dr. Tampa, FL 33610

The River at Tampa Bay Church was founded on December 1, 1996. At the close of 1996, the Lord planted within Pastors Rodney and Adonica's heart the vision and desire to start a church in Tampa. With a heart for the lost and to minister to those who had been touched by revival, they implemented that vision and began The River at Tampa Bay, with the motto, "Church with a Difference."

Over 500 people joined them for the first Sunday morning service on December 1, 1996. Over the years, the membership has grown and the facilities have changed, yet these three things have remained constant since the church's inception... dynamic praise and worship, anointed preaching and teaching of the Word, and powerful demonstrations of the Holy Spirit and power. The Lord spoke to Pastor Rodney's heart to feed the people, touch the people, and love the people. With this in mind and heart, the goal of the River is:

- To become a model revival church where people from all over the world can come and be touched by God. Once they have been not only touched, but changed, they are ready to be launched out into the harvest field with the anointing of God.
- To have a church that is multi-racial, representing a cross section of society from rich to poor from all nations, bringing people to a place of maturity in their Christian walk.
- To see the lost, the backslidden and the unsure come to a full assurance of their salvation.
- To be a home base for Revival Ministries International and all of its arms. A base offering strength and support to

the vision of RMI to see America shaken with the fires of revival, then to take that fire to the far-flung corners of the globe.

- To break the mold of religious tradition and thinking.
- To be totally dependent upon the Holy Spirit for His leading and guidance as we lead others deeper into the River of God.
- Our motto: Church with a Difference.

For The River at Tampa Bay's service times and directions, please, visit revival.com or call 1 (813) 971-9999.

The River Bible Institute

The River Bible Institute (RBI) is a place where men and women of all ages, backgrounds and experiences can gather together to study and experience the glory of God. The River Bible Institute is not a traditional Bible school. It is a Holy Ghost training center, birthed specifically for those whose strongest desire is to know Christ and to make Him known.

The vision for The River Bible Institute is plain: To train men and women in the spirit of revival for ministry in the 21st century. The school was birthed in 1997 with a desire to train up revivalists for the 21st Century. It is a place where the Word of God and the Holy Spirit come together to produce life, birth ministries, and launch them out. The River Bible Institute is a place where ministries are sent to the far-flung corners of the globe to spread revival and to bring in a harvest of souls for the kingdom of God.

While preaching in many nations and regions of the world, Dr. Rodney Howard-Browne has observed that all the people of the earth have one thing in common: A desperate need for the genuine touch of God. From the interior of Alaska through the bush country of Africa, to the outback villages of Australia to the cities of North America, people are tired of religion and ritualistic worship. They are crying out for the reality of His presence. The River Bible Institute is dedicated to training believers how to live, minister, and flow in the anointing.

The Word will challenge those attending the Institute to find clarity in their calling, and be changed by the awesome presence of God. This is the hour of God's power. Not just for the full-time minister, but for all of God's people who are hungry for more. Whether you are a housewife or an aspiring evangelist, The River Bible Institute will deepen your relationship and experience in the Lord, and provide you with a new perspective on how to reach others with God's life-changing power.

You can be saturated in the Word and the Spirit of God at The River Bible Institute. It is the place where you will be empowered to reach your high calling and set your world on fire with revival.

For more information about the River Bible Institute, please, visit revival.com or call 1 (813) 899-0085 or 1 (813) 971-9999.

The River School of Worship

The River School of Worship (RSW) is where ability becomes accountability, talent becomes anointing and ambition becomes vision.

It has been Drs. Rodney and Adonica Howard-Browne's dream for many years to provide a place where men and women of all ages, backgrounds and experiences could gather together to study and experience the glory of God. The River School of Worship is not a traditional music school. It is a training center birthed specifically for those whose strongest desire is to worship in Spirit and in Truth, and where the Word of God and the Holy Spirit come together to produce life, birth ministries, and launch them out.

The Word will challenge those of you attending to find clarity in your calling, and be changed by the awesome presence of God. The River School of Worship will deepen your relationship and experience in the Lord, and provide you with a new perspective on how to reach others with God's life-changing power. You can be saturated in the Word and the Spirit of God at the River School of Worship. It is the place where you will be empowered to reach your high calling and set your world on fire with Revival.

For more information about the River School of Worship, please, visit revival.com or call 1 (813) 899-0085 or 1 (813) 971-9999.

The River School of Government

Moreover, you shall choose able men from all the people — God-fearing men of truth who hate unjust gain — and place them over thousands, hundreds, fifties, and tens, to be their rulers. Exodus 18:21 AMP

The River School of Government (RSG) has been founded as a result of the corruption we see in the current government system and the need to raise up godly individuals with personal and public integrity to boldly take up positions of leadership in our nation. For hundreds of years the Constitution of the United States of America, the supreme law of the land, has stood as a bulwark of righteousness, to protect the rights of its citizens. However, there have been attacks, from many quarters, all designed to neutralize the Constitution and to progressively remove citizens' rights.

There is a great need to raise up individuals who will run for office in the United States of America, from the very bottom all the way to the highest level of government, who will honor and stand up for both the integrity of the Constitution and the integrity of God's Word. If we are going to see America changed for the good, we have to get back to her founding principles, which were laid out by the Founding Fathers at her inception. This is the heart and soul and primary focus of the River School of Government.

The River School of Government will work to expose the enemies of our sovereignty and Constitution. The student will be trained in every area of governmental leadership and responsibility, and upon successful graduation will be entrusted with specific positions, tasks and responsibilities, each according to their ability and calling. The River School of Government's goal is not to raise up career politicians, who will abuse their position for personal gain or for personal power, but to raise up people who will govern according to solid godly principles and who will continue to faithfully defend the individual rights and freedoms that are guaranteed by both the Constitution and God's Word.

The River School of Government is non-partisan and has one objective – to raise up people in government, who are armed with a solid foundation in the Constitution, God's Holy Word, and the power of the Holy Spirit - to take America back! We believe that the Lord will help us to accomplish this goal of taking America back, with a well-defined four, eight, twelve, sixteen, and twenty-year plan, springing out of a third Great Spiritual Awakening!

For more information about the River School of Government, please, call 1 (813) 899-0085 or1 (813) 971-9999 or email us at rsg@revival.com

God Wants to Use You to Bring in the Harvest of Souls!

The Great Commission, "Go ye into all the world and preach the gospel to every creature," is for every believer to take personally. Every believer is to be an announcer of the Good News Gospel. When the Gospel is preached, people have an encounter with Jesus. Jesus is the only One Who can change the heart of a man, woman, child, and nation! On the next page is a tool to assist you in sharing the Gospel with others. It is called the Gospel Soul Winning Script. Please, just read it! Read it to others and you will see many come to Christ because, as stated in Romans 1:16, the Gospel is the power of God.

Please, visit revival.com, click on Soul-winning Tools, and review the many tools and videos that are freely available to help you bring in the harvest of souls. It's harvest time!

THE GOSPEL SOUL-WINNING —SCRIPT—

Has anyone ever told you that God loves you and that He has a wonderful plan for your life? I have a real quick, but important question to ask you. If you were to die this very second, do you know for sure, beyond a shadow of a doubt, that you would go to Heaven? [If "Yes"— Great, why would you say "Yes"? (If they respond with anything but "I have Jesus in my heart" or something similar to that, PROCEED WITH SCRIPT) or "No" or "I hope so" PROCEED WITH SCRIPT.]

Let me quickly share with you what the Holy Bible reads. It reads "for all have sinned and come short of the glory of God" and "for the wages of sin is death, but the gift of God is eternal life through Jesus Christ our Lord". The Bible also reads, "For whosoever shall call upon the name of the Lord shall be saved". And you're a "whosoever" right? Of course you are; all of us are.

continued on reverse side—

JESUS SAVES • JESUS HEALS • JESUS DELIVERS

I'm going to say a quick prayer for you. Lord, bless (FILL IN NAME) and his/her family with long and healthy lives. Jesus, make Yourself real to him/her and do a quick work in his/her heart. If (FILL IN NAME) has not received Jesus Christ as his/her Lord and Savior, I pray he/she will do so now.

(FILL IN NAME), if you would like to receive the gift that God has for you today, say this after me with your heart and lips out loud. Dear Lord Jesus, come into my heart. Forgive me of my sin. Wash me and cleanse me. Set me free. Jesus, thank You that You died for me. I believe that You are risen from the dead and that You're coming back again for me. Fill me with the Holy Spirit. Give me a passion for the lost, a hunger for the things of God and a holy boldness to preach the gospel of Jesus Christ. I'm saved; I'm born again, I'm forgiven and I'm on my way to Heaven because I have Jesus in my heart.

As a minister of the gospel of Jesus Christ, I tell you today that all of your sins are forgiven. Always remember to run to God and not from God because He loves you and has a great plan for your life.

[Invite them to your church and get follow up info: name, address, & phone number.]

Revival Ministries International
P.O. Box 292888 • Tampa, FL 33687
(813) 971-9999 • www.revival.com